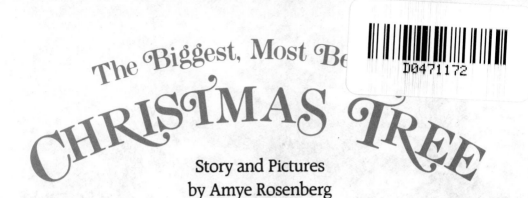

The Biggest, Most Beautiful CHRISTMAS TREE

Story and Pictures
by Amye Rosenberg

A GOLDEN BOOK • NEW YORK

Western Publishing Company, Inc., Racine, Wisconsin 53404

Nestled deep in a thick forest, there was a great fir tree. Animals made cozy homes in the sturdy trunk.

Mr. and Mrs. Fieldmouse lived downstairs. Old Gray Acorn, the squirrel, lived upstairs. And in between dwelt the Chipmunk family—Mom, Dad, Little Nina, and Nutley.

Life in the big fir tree was happy all year round.
But when Christmas came, the tree animals always
felt sad. And the Chipmunk children were saddest of
all.

Every year they baked special Christmas cookies.
They hung up stockings and waited for Santa to fill
them with goodies. But Santa never came.

This year the children were sadder than ever. So
Mom and Dad Chipmunk decided to give a Christmas
party to cheer them up. They invited all the
neighbors and their favorite aunt, Mim.

Aunt Mim arrived with a big sack and a big smile, but the children were not cheerful.

"It's nearly Christmas!" boomed Aunt Mim. "Why are you so glum?"

Little Nina sadly explained. "Every year we bake cookies," she said. "We hang our stockings. We wait for Santa. But he never comes."

"We think he doesn't like us," sniffled Nutley

"Nonsense!" declared Aunt Mim, who was very wise. "He probably doesn't even know you are here, tucked away in this huge tree. Why, from his sleigh up in the sky, your home looks like just another tree in the forest. I have an idea, and you all must help."

The children's eyes sparkled with hope.

Aunt Mim began to empty her sack. There were huge bolts of red ribbon, a big roll of gold foil, and balloons and berries and bells that jingled.

"Now!" said Aunt Mim. "Let's go outside and turn this big old fir tree into the biggest, most beautiful Christmas tree in the world, so Santa can't miss it. Hurry! Tonight is Christmas Eve!"

They all scampered out onto the snowy branches,
carrying the things from Aunt Mim's sack.

Mom began to tie bows on all the fir cones. The little Chipmunks snipped the ends.

Dad was up top, fashioning a big gold star out of foil.

Old Gray Acorn busily blew up balloons and tied them to the branches. Then Mr. and Mrs. Fieldmouse painted dots, stars, and candy-cane stripes on the balloons.

Little Nina and Nutley helped by painting a funny Santa on one red balloon. It made everyone giggle.

Aunt Mim ran strings of berries up and down and all around the tree. "Hurry!" she urged. "It's getting late!"

Little Nina munched a few berries when Aunt Mim wasn't looking.

The others hung jingle bells that tinkled gleefully when the branches shook. Nutley jumped up and down to make sure of that!

When Dad's gold star was placed on top, the tree was finished. It glowed in the moonlight. All the animals of the forest came to admire it.

"Ours is truly the biggest, most beautiful Christmas tree in the world!" exclaimed Little Nina and Nutley.

"Santa will surely find you now!" Aunt Mim said with a laugh.

Everyone went to bed early that night. They were tired from their hard work.

Old Gray Acorn fell asleep in his big easy chair.

Mr. and Mrs. Fieldmouse snuggled under their warm quilt.

Mom and Dad snoozed in their nightcaps, and Aunt Mim snored by the stove.

The littlest Chipmunks fell asleep without even touching their hot cocoa.

The children awoke early to find the house filled with toys and gifts. Their stockings bulged with goodies.

"It worked!" shrieked the children, dancing up and down. "Santa has found us at last! Hooray! Hooray!"

Their joyous squeals roused everyone.

The neighbors heard them and arrived with gifts of their own.

"After all these years," declared Old Gray Acorn, "Christmas has come to this old tree."

Dad brought out special Christmas cookies and tea, and the children shared the goodies with their friends. Everyone raised a cup and drank a toast to Christmas—and to wise Aunt Mim, who just smiled her big smile.

Thanks to her, Santa would always find the animals' tiny homes in the biggest, most beautiful Christmas tree in the world.